WELCOME TO
PASSPORT TO READING
A beginning reader's ticket to a brand-new world!

Every book in this program is designed to build read-along and read-alone skills, level by level, through engaging and enriching stories. As the reader turns each page, he or she will become more confident with new vocabulary, sight words, and comprehension.

These PASSPORT TO READING levels will help you choose the perfect book for every reader.

READING TOGETHER
Read short words in simple sentence structures together to begin a reader's journey.

READING OUT LOUD
Encourage developing readers to sound out words in more complex stories with simple vocabulary.

READING INDEPENDENTLY
Newly independent readers gain confidence reading more complex sentences with higher word counts.

READY TO READ MORE
Readers prepare for chapter books with fewer illustrations and longer paragraphs.

This book features sight words from the educator-supported Dolch Sight Words List. This encourages the reader to recognize commonly used vocabulary words, increasing reading speed and fluency.

For more information, please visit passporttoreadingbooks.com

Enjoy the jou...

Alien Mix-Up

Adapted by Lauren Forte

Based on the episode "Kitchen Whizz"

written by Tim Bain

LITTLE, BROWN AND COMPANY

New York   Boston

Attention, Bob the Builder fans!
Look for these words
when you read this book.
Can you spot them all?

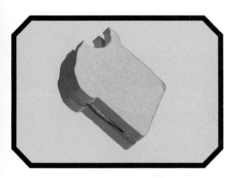

sandwich

backpack

paint

alien

"Can I fix lunch?

Yes, I can!"

said Bob the Builder.

He put sandwiches in his backpack.

Pilchard jumped onto the counter.
Then she jumped into the backpack.
Bob did not notice.

Bob and the team went to
The Flying Saucepan restaurant.
They had a job to do!

"It looks like a spaceship," Scoop said.

"That is the idea!" said Bob.

Chef Tattie arrived with crates
of ingredients.

He was going to make a delicious meal
to serve at the restaurant that night!

First there was a job to do!

Scoop and Muck hauled rocks.

Leo painted the rocks green.

"An alien could live here," said Leo.

"What is an alien?" Lofty asked.
"Aliens are little green visitors
from other planets," Leo answered.
"What do they look like?" Muck asked.

"They have three eyes
and four legs," said Leo.
He painted an alien on a rock
to show Muck.

No one noticed Pilchard climbing out of the backpack.

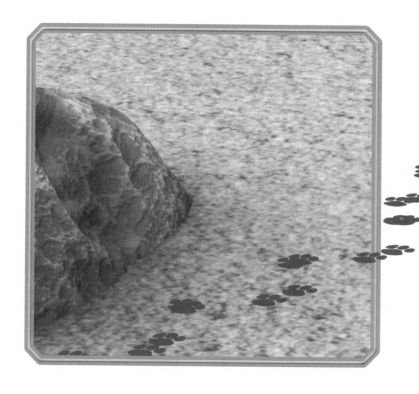

She jumped down and

landed in the tray of green paint.

Then she walked away.

She left a trail of green paw prints.

Time for lunch!

Leo took the backpack

and headed up to the restaurant.

"Look!" Muck shouted,
as he spotted the green paw prints.
"It must be an alien!"

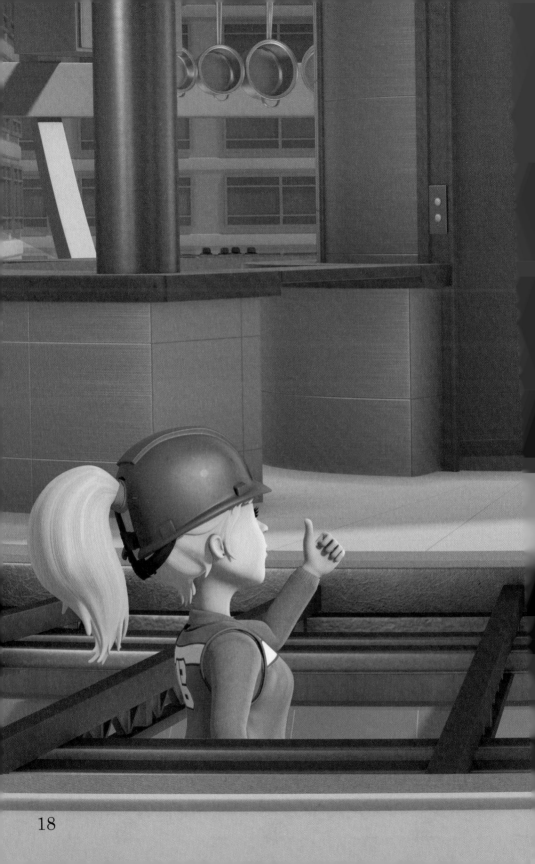

Inside the restaurant, Wendy hooked up a motor to the floor. "Want to take it for a test spin?" she asked.

"This remote changes the speed,"
Wendy said, hitting the button.

The floor began to move!
"Bravo!" shouted Chef Tattie.

Leo stepped out of the elevator and gave Bob the backpack.

"I hope everyone is hungry!" said Bob.

But the backpack was nearly empty!
"Someone ate our lunch!"
declared Bob.

Downstairs, Pilchard wandered
into the elevator.
The doors closed.

The vehicles heard the elevator moving.

"The alien is in there!" shouted Muck.

When Pilchard reached the restaurant,
she jumped onto a bench.
Then she curled up on the remote.

Suddenly, the floor began to move faster!

Everyone grabbed on to a table.

"Pilchard is on the remote!" yelled Bob.

"Pilchard, do you want dinner?"
Bob called.

Pilchard jumped off the remote.

"Phew," they all said as the floor
slowed down.